-the- PIRATE KIDS

The Great Treasure Hunt

BY Johanna Gohmann

ILLUSTRATED BY Jessika von Innerebner

Calico Kid

An Imprint of Magic Wagon

abdopublishing.com

For Lissy – A treasured teacher. Thank you for every little story you read, and every little book you made. —JG

To CA who is always up for adventure. —JV

abdopublishing.com

Published by Magic Wagon, a division of ABDO, PO Box 398166, Minneapolis, Minnesota 55439.

Printed in the United States of America, North Mankato, Minnesota.
082017
012018

Written by Johanna Gohmann
Illustrated by Jessika von Innerebner
Edited by Heidi M.D. Elston
Art Directed by Candice Keimig

Publisher's Cataloging in Publication Data

Names: Gohmann, Johanna, author. | von Innerebner, Jessika, illustrator.
Title: The great treasure hunt / by Johanna Gohmann; illustrated by Jessika von Innerebner.
Description: Minneapolis, Minnesota : Magic Wagon, 2018. | Series: The pirate kids
Summary: Piper and Percy have been arguing all day. Then their parents give them a map and drop them off on a secret island for their first treasure hunt. They have to work together! Piper and Percy swim in a waterfall, play with a monkey, and laugh together. But they don't find the treasure. At the end of the day, their parents tell them they did find the treasure - friendship.
Identifiers: LCCN 2017946451 | ISBN 9781532130397 (lib.bdg.) | ISBN 9781532130991 (ebook) | ISBN 9781532131295 (Read-to-me ebook)
Subjects: LCSH: Pirates--Fiction--Juvenile fiction. | Brothers and sisters--Juvenile fiction. | Orienteering--Juvenile fiction. | Friendship--Juvenile fiction.
Classification: DDC [E]--dc23
LC record available at https://lccn.loc.gov/2017946451

Table of Contents

Chapter #1

Two Grumpy Pirates

"It's my turn to feed Poppy!" Piper shouts at her little brother.

"You fed her yesterday!" Percy yells back. He stomps across the kitchen and pours seed into her dish.

"That's not fair!" Piper says, grabbing for the box of seeds.

Suddenly, tiny seeds scatter all over the kitchen. Some of them even land in their father's coffee mug.

"Argh!" says their father.

"Argh!" says Poppy the parrot, who sits balanced on their father's shoulder.

“I take milk and sugar in my coffee, not birdseed!” their dad says.

“Sorry,” Percy says.

“I think you little mateys woke up on the wrong side of the ship this morning.”

Piper and Percy frown at each other.

"Clean up this mess. Then why don't ye go play above deck?"

"Okay," Piper says.

Piper and Percy clean up the mess. But first, they argue over who should hold the broom. And they fight over who should hold the dustpan.

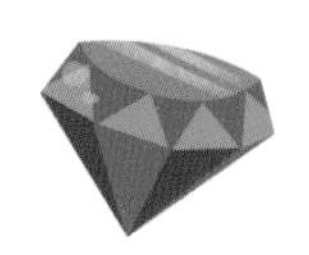

Above deck, Percy asks Piper what she'd like to play. But Piper is already sitting in a hammock. She's holding a large ruby up to the sun.

"Isn't it sparkly in the light?" Piper says.

"Hey, wait a minute!" Percy shouts. "That's the ruby Mom brought me from her last treasure hunt!"

“No, this one is mine,” Piper says.

“It’s mine! See? It has a tiny crack at the top.” Percy tries to grab the jewel from his sister. But she holds it out of his reach.

“You think everything is yours!” Piper yells. “I’m tired of it!”

"Well, I'm tired of you," Percy says with a scowl.

"Oh, why don't you go walk the plank," Piper says.

"Children!" their mother calls. She walks over to them, her hands on her hips. "What is all of this fighting about?"

Chapter #2

An Exciting Surprise

"She stole my treasure!" Percy points at Piper.

"I did not! It's my treasure!" Piper frowns.

"Aye, I think now it will be *my* treasure," their mother says. "Hand it over, please."

Piper sighs then hands the ruby to her mother.

"How would you like to find some new treasure?" their mother asks.

Piper and Percy look at each other.

"What do you mean?" Percy asks.

"Well," their mother says, "your father and I think you're ready for your first treasure hunt. We're dropping you off on Bluebeard Island today."

"All by ourselves?" Piper asks.

"Yes." Their mother smiles.

"Our very first treasure hunt, brother!" Piper grins.

"Shiver me timbers!" Percy jumps with excitement.

"Here's your map," their mother says, holding out a piece of yellow paper. Piper and Percy both reach for it at the same time.

"I want to hold it!" Percy says.

"No, you're terrible at map reading!" Piper says.

They both tug on the map.

Rrrriiiipppp!

The map tears right down the middle.

Their mother shakes her head. "Aye, you two won't have much luck if you can't figure out how to work together. Come along now. We're almost there."

Chapter #3

Island Fun

Piper and Percy stand on the shore of Bluebeard Island. Their mom and dad wave to them from the deck of their ship.

“Have fun, my little mateys!” their father calls.

“We’ll be back later this afternoon!” Their mother smiles down at them. “Remember, work together!”

The children watch the ship sail away. They've never been alone on an island before.

"It's pretty here, isn't it?" Piper says.

Percy pulls off his pirate boots and stands in the soft sand. "Argh, that feels nice!"

Percy picks up a coconut and cracks it open with his wooden sword. He takes a big drink of the milk inside.

"Yum!" He grins.

"Percy, we aren't here to play in the sand and eat coconuts. We're here to find treasure," Piper says.

“Okay,” Percy grumbles. “But would you like to have a drink first?”

“Really?” Piper asks. “You’ll share it with me?”

Percy holds the coconut out to his sister. Just then, a small brown monkey darts in front of him. It swipes the coconut right out of Percy’s hand!

"Yo ho ho!" the children laugh together.

"What a silly monkey!" Piper says. "Thanks for trying to share it with me though. Here, why don't we put our pieces of the map back together and see if we can figure out where to go?"

The children each hold up their piece of the map.

"I think if we head this way, it will lead to the waterfall. It looks like the treasure might be there?" Percy wonders. "I know I'm not very good at map reading."

Piper smiles at him.

"You know what little brother, I think you're right! Let's walk toward the waterfall!"

Chapter #4

The Best Treasure of All

Piper and Percy follow the map to a beautiful, tumbling waterfall. All around them are brightly colored birds and giant flowers.

"Wow! What a place!" Percy says.

"You did a great job reading the map," Piper says. "C'mon, let's go for a swim."

The children carefully hang their black hats and pirate patches in a tree.

They both laugh as they jump into the water. The waterfall tumbles down around them. They take turns jumping off a big rock.

"Percy, look," Piper says. "Our monkey friend is back."

"Hey!" Percy shouts. "He's got my pirate hat!"

The children giggle as the monkey swings through the trees, wearing Percy's hat.

"I guess he wants to be a pirate, too," Piper says.

"Argh, a monkey pirate!" Percy laughs.

Suddenly, Piper and Percy's parents appear beside the waterfall.

"I see you found the famous Bluebeard Falls." Their father winks at them.

"We did!" Piper says. "And it's been as fun as a barrel of doubloons!"

"But," Percy frowns, "I'm afraid we didn't find the treasure."

“Argh, my little mateys. But you did,” their father says.

“Huh?” Piper is puzzled. “We did?”

“But of course you did.” Their mother smiles. “Real treasure doesn’t come in a treasure chest, children. The real treasure in life is friendship!”

Piper and Percy grin at each other.

"Then we both have a lot of treasure. Right, sister?" Percy says.

Piper playfully splashes him. "We sure do, brother."